So, what do I do with this?

www.LookingGreat.Today   2018

Bea Marshall

1

So, what do I do with this?

At 39 most of us went to bed slim, firm and gorgeous, we knew what fit and what suited us, we could walk into a shop and grab something from the rail, confident it would fit and look alright. Then we woke up at 40 with a face and body that we didn't recognise and have no idea what to do with. Don't despair, I can help. Read on....

Authors Note:

This book has been put together from a myriad of sources, with the intention of helping women to look in the mirror and feel fabulous.

It has been many years in the making, starting as an idea in a tiny shop in Woodville New Zealand, then completed whilst diligently (ehem!) studying for my Degree and running my makeover business in the UK.   I help to make women of all shapes and sizes feel absolutely gorgeous again by running courses as well as one to one sessions, but I also wanted women to have something they could hold, write in and refer back to. This book is intended as a guide that you can make notes in, dip in and out of and astound your friends with your knowledge of yours and their body shapes.

So, here is my book, cleverly called... "So, what do I do with this?" which I hope that you enjoy.

Contents

Introduction

As we grow older, our body shape and personal preferences change. What suited us when we were 16 may not still look good at 46. The colours and styles we love, don't seem to love us back so much. But dressing our new age and body can be very tricky and leave us feeling frustrated. This personal guide, designed just for women over forty, is here to help you through the rough bits and give you the solid, basic information to hang your new wardrobe and confidence on. When it comes to looking good, it's not your size or shape that matters, it is the fit of your clothes and choosing what suits you and helps you to feel confident.

This guide will help you to:

- Discover your body frame and how to dress it.
- Build confidence in your ability to make the most of your assets whilst accentuating the positive in your new choices.
- Create a balanced, confident look.
- Examine your clothing personality and how you present yourself to the world
- Develop a better understanding of your own, unique, style.
- Put together all you have learned.

Your Horizontal Body Type

Most of us are unhappy with our body shape for one reason or another. However, whether you like your body or not, if you understand what your current shape and proportions are and know a few style guidelines for your shape, you are well on your way to looking and feeling like your best self.

The female body types most people are familiar with are what image consultants refer to as the horizontal body shapes. These are:

- Hourglass
- Inverted triangle (also referred to as a cone, wedge or v shape)
- Rectangle (also called the ruler, the brick, lean or the straight body)
- Apple
- Pear

Your horizontal shape is important for the clothing silhouettes and design elements that will book best on you. However, the other important proportion is your vertical body type. There are 3 of these: short legs, long body - balanced body - and long legs short body.

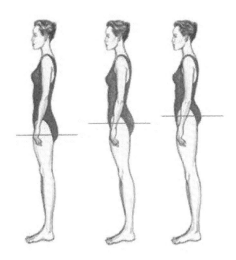

Short Legs Long Body   Balanced Body   Long Legs Short Body

The Female Vertical Body Proportions:

Your vertical proportion is important for the lengths of clothes (both for tops and for bottoms) that will be most flattering on you.

However, for your most flattering styles, you also need to take other aspects of your body into account. These include:

- Your **face shape**
- Your weight
- Your height
- Your **bone structure**
- Your shoulder size and angle
- Your neck length and circumference
- Your age
- Your health
- Any figure variations such as a large bottom, a large stomach, or saddle bags

Let's get started by assessing your vertical body type and your horizontal body type.

What is the Perfect Shape?

Luckily beauty is in the eye of the beholder. However, the current thinking for the ideal female body shape, is moderately tall with a body balanced vertically, therefore an hourglass figure along with an oval shaped face.

For males the ideal is tall with a balanced vertical body and a trapezoid torso (that is, broad shoulders and chest tapering to medium waist and hips) and an oval face. However, this book is primarily for women, so we will concentrate primarily on the female body shape throughout the book.

So, You Don't Have the Ideal Shape?

Not many of us do (only something like 2% of the population). However, you can create the impression of a perfect body by choosing clothes to create the illusion of the ideal proportions. It's all about balancing your perceived shape to the ideal shape (or moving your appearance in that direction, anyway).

For example, as a female, if you have long legs and a short, rectangle torso you can create the look of a longer, leaner, inverted triangle torso (the next best female shape). Do this by choosing tops that emphasize your shoulders and that flow through the waist, with a hemline between the lower hip to

the tip of your fingers and with no horizontal seams across your torso.

As a male, if you have short legs and a long rectangle torso you can create the illusion of longer legs and a shorter trapezoid body by choosing shirts that make your shoulders look wider and tuck in your shirt to make your torso look shorter (as long as your stomach isn't too big). Choose trousers that are darker than your shirt and shoes in the same colour as your trousers, or darker, to make your legs look longer.

Changing Shape

Of course, understanding your current shape doesn't rule out your shape changing through diet and exercise or, more drastically, through health issues or even plastic surgery. The idea is to make the most of whatever shape you are now.

If you do change shape by more than 5.5cm (2 inches) then you should re-assess your body shape and ensure your clothing choices still flatter your current shape.

Determine Your Vertical Body Type

Start by assessing your vertical body proportions. This is the proportion of the bottom half of your body compared to your top half.

Vertical shape is important for identifying your best garment lengths (tops and bottoms) and will come into play in

determining if you should tuck-in tops or wear top garments un-tucked for example.

There are three vertical body types, and these are applicable to both males and females.

The most accurate way to determine your vertical shape is to measure your full height and the height to your low hip-line (your low hip-line is the circumference around your hips where your bottom is fullest) and determine where your hip-line comes in relation to your height.

Alternatively use the following rough assessment guidelines...

Short Legs, Long Torso

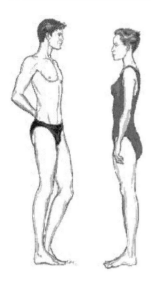

If your legs are short compared to your upper body you have short legs and a long torso...

- Your hip-line height is less than half your height
- You may also have a low waist -- your waist will be lower than your bent elbow
- You will have a long torso -- typically you will put on weight first on your thighs and hips
- Your bottom will typically be low and heavy
- You may also be short -- although tall people can also be short legged

Your main style aims are to create the illusion of longer legs and a shorter torso.

Do wear...

- Jewellery, scarves and garment designs that draw the observer's eye up towards your shoulders and face
- Short to medium-long tops
- Tucked-in tops (if slim)
- Layered tops
- Medium or light tops and dark trousers or skirts

- Medium to wide belts
- Straight skirts
- Straight or boot-leg pants
- Trouser, sock and shoe colours the same
- Medium to high heels
- Trouser hems to the ground

Don't wear...

- Long tops (if you are short)
- Trousers or skirts with a dropped waistband
- Tight or tapered skirts
- Tight or tapered trousers
- Cropped trousers

Balanced Body

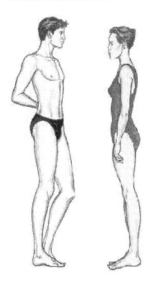

If your upper body length is about the same as your lower body length you have a balanced body...

- Your hip-line height is half your full height
- Your waist is at your bent elbow
- Females may be low busted
- You tend to put on weight around your torso or hips and thighs
- You may have a round well-formed bottom or you may have a flat bottom
- You have proportionally slim arms and legs

If you are less than 160cm (5'3") with a small to **medium body scale** then you are also petite.

Your main style aim is to elongate your mid-torso.

Do wear...

- Jewellery, scarves and garment designs that draw the observer's eye up towards your shoulders and face
- Medium-long tops
- Un-tucked tops
- Tops and bottoms in the same colour
- Tops and dresses that flow through the waist
- Skirts and trousers with narrow waistbands or no waistband
- Straight or flared skirts
- Waisted, low-rise or hipster trousers
- Straight or flared trousers

Don't wear...

- Short tops
- Empire line tops and dresses
- Wide belts
- Trousers or skirts with a high waistband

Long Legs, Short Torso

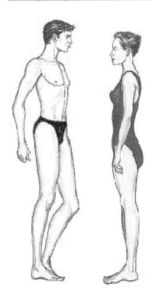

If your legs are longer than your upper body you have a long legged vertical body type...

- Your hipline height is higher than half your full height
- You should also have a high waist -- your waist will be higher than your bent elbow
- You will have a proportionally short torso
- Your bottom will typically be round and high
- You tend to put on weight around your waist, above your waist or on the back of your hips
- You may also be tall -- although short people can also be long legged

Your main style aims are to create visual balance by creating the illusion of a longer mid-torso and shorter legs.

Do wear...

- Design details that draw the eye down, such as border prints on skirts and trousers (unless you are short)
- Medium-long to long accessories (unless you are short)
- Skirts and trousers in the lighter colours than tops
- Medium-long to long tops (if you are short, no longer than knuckle length)
- Un-tucked tops
- Tops and dresses that flow through the waist
- Skirts and trousers with narrow waistbands or no waistband
- Straight and flared skirts
- Low-rise or hipster trousers
- Straight and flared trousers

Don't wear...

- Focal points that draw the eye upwards
- Pin stripes
- Short tops
- Empire line tops and dresses
- Wide belts
- Trousers or skirts with a high waistband
- Tapered trousers and skirts

Figure Analysis

Despite the media's best efforts, please believe that there is no 'ideal' size or shape. Every single one of us is perfect.

Your Shape:

Face shape ■ square ■ oval ■ heart

Height: Short ■ medium ■ tall   _____ cms

Neck length ■ short ■ average ■ long   _____ cms

Shoulders ■ narrow ■ proportional ■ wide   _____ cms

Bust ■ small ■ average ■ full ■ low ■ high   _____ cms

Arm length ■ short ■ average ■ long   _____ cms

Waist ■ small ■ average ■ thick   _____ cms

Tummy ■ flat ■ protruding ■ large

Hips ■ narrow ■ proportional ■ wide ■ heavy   _____ cms

Bottom ■ round ■ flat ■ average ■ broad

Legs ■ short ■ proportioned ■ long ■ heavy ■ slim ■ proportional

Torso ■ short ■ proportioned ■ long ■ mid-framed

Bone structure ■ small ■ medium ■ large

Frame ....

Figure Analysis... Pear

- You carry weight at the hips or thighs
- Have narrower shoulders than hips
- Have a clearly defined waist
- Wear a larger size on your bottom half than your top.

If you have lost and gained weight often, your body shape may change into another. You can lean toward an hourglass if your bust is heavier or an apple if your weight gain goes to your bottom and thighs.

Corrective measures:

- You need to balance your top and lower half by wearing clothes that make your shoulders look broader.
- Jackets and tops need to finish either above or below the widest point of your hips and bottom, not at the widest point.
- Balance the top with your fuller bottom half. Layering on your top half creates visual interest and draws the eye upward.
- Wear volume, clutter, colour and pattern on your top half.
- Wear fitted styles around your waist and accentuate your waistline with empire lines and wraps.
- Make your shoulders look wider with padded shoulders, puffed sleeves, capped sleeves or boleros.

Avoid:

- Narrowing leg trousers like cigarette trousers, pleats or creases in your leg-line, pin stripe suits, turn-ups, wide or flared leg trousers, combats or cropped trousers and culottes.
- Detail, patterns or pockets in the thigh and hip area.
- Belts worn on the hip.
- Straight or pencil skirts.
- Bags that sit across your hips.
- Ankle straps, kitten heels, Uggs, round toes, ankle boots and straps around your calf.
- Any hemline that finishes on your hips.
- Double vent jackets.
- Dropped waistlines.
- Sloping or narrowed shoulder lines.

Try to choose from the following lists, to compliment your shape.

Neckline:

You are pretty lucky here and can wear

- wide collars
- Boat necks
- Crew necks

- Bardot
- Lapels

Sleeves:

- Cap
- ¾ length
- Dropped
- Batwing
- Puffed
- Above or below wrist
- Short sleeves.

Tops and shirts:

- Wear fitted shapes:
  - Wrap tops
  - Empire
  - Vests
  - Waistcoats
  - Stiff fabrics / straight yokes
  - Hoods
  - Back yokes
  - Back belts

Coats:

- Trench coats
- Big lapels
- Wide collars

- Double breasted
- Detailed at top, simple below

- Fitted shapes
- Belted

Dresses:

Empire lines and wrap dresses look great on you, separates look even better.

Skirts:

- Straight tapered knee length
- Bias cut
- Mid-calf

Trousers:

- Plain
- Flat fronted
- Bootleg & flares if tall
- Ankle length
- Simple, no belt loops, braces, pleats, pockets, turn ups.

Shoes:

- Medium to chunky heel
- Wedges
- Single coloured knee boots
- Neutral colours
- Pointed or square toe.

Bags

Choose a bag that sits at your waist. Detail, chunky, patterned or embellished. Or choose a clutch bag.

Swim-wear

Keep all detailing above the waist. Beware of cuts that finish at your widest point. Separates work well but keep the lower half one colour, preferably neutral.

Notes:

Lines & Shapes

Congratulations, you are hippy and hip. You share the same body shape with the likes of Beyoncé, Kim Kardashian, Eva Longoria and Paris Hilton.

Style challenges include finding clothing items that fit both your waist (tiny) and your hips (a bit wider). Dresses can be a challenge because slim-cut fashion may not flare enough to accommodate the bottom half of your **pear-shaped body**, while remaining tailored to the top half of your body.

- Focus attention upward. Pear-shaped women should focus attention on the upper half of their pear-shaped body by choosing slim, fitted tops, button-down shirts and cardigans.
- Embellish around the neck. Shirts and dresses with embellished necklines naturally draw the eye upward toward the slimmest part of a pear-shaped body.
- Layer it up. Layering garments can balance a pear-shaped body by adding visual interest to the top half of the body.
- Go for an A. A-line dresses and tops emphasize the upper body while slimming wider hips characteristic of a pear-shaped body.
- Wide is good. Keep the hems of pants, skirts and dresses wide to visually balance a pear-shaped body. Pointy-toed shoes with a wide-hemmed pants will elongate your legs.
- Get a little structure. Structured pants are a great fit, especially those that skim the hips and thighs of a
- pear-shaped body. Avoid flashy embellishments like cargo pants, funky pockets or embroidery.

Flirty skirts for Pears

The right skirt can show off your assets and hide any figure flaws. Check out these skirt suggestions for pear body shapes:

Conceal with a subtle print, says fashion experts. A small-scale texture like dark tweed or any other shaded fabric can hide any little bulge.

A slightly flared pencil skirt shows off legs while still camouflaging thighs. The top-of-knee length elongates your lower half.

Note these skirt fashion tips for pears.

- o   Do learn to love a slight A-line.
- o   Do pick a style that sits at your waist or hips but doesn't go super high.
- o   Do keep it simple – nothing too shiny or glitzy.
- o   Avoid allover tight skirts. They'll make you bottom-heavy.

Looking at Tops:

Carrying weight on the bottom half is a challenge for dressing -- but if you keep your focus on highlighting the top of your body, you'll show off your beautifully curvy body in its best light.

- •   Show off your collarbone. Play up this very attractive part of your body to draw attention to the neck and face area, and away from your bottom half.

- •   Opt for a blazer. One of the most enduring, classic trends is a strong shoulder such as that of a blazer. Leave out the shoulder pads from the 1980s and instead go for fuller jackets and blazers with clean and interesting lines.

- •   Go for patterns & light colors on top. Pear-shaped bodies look great in patterned and light tops paired with dark and denim on the bottom.

Casual dresses for pears

Dresses with A-line or flared skirts look fabulous on pears.

A halter dress will make your shoulders appear wider, helping to balance out your hips and thighs. A shirt dress is a great option, too. It's casual yet chic, and the neckline draws the attention upwards.

Notes:

Figure Analysis... Apple

You have a rounded bust, waist, tummy and hip. Your legs are usually nicely proportioned and shapely and you probably feel uncomfortable tucking tops in.

You have:

- Rounder shoulder line
- Flattish bottom
- Average to large bust
- Fuller around the middle

If you have gained and lost weight, your body shape may tend to change into another one. If your hips are slightly larger (saddle bags), then you are leaning toward a Pear shape.   Shoulders slightly broader than your hips? Then you are tending toward an Inverted Triangle. If you lose weight around your tummy, you may gain a waist and lean toward an hourglass.

Corrective measures:

Avoid wearing:

- Sleeves finishing near the bust
- Above the knee skirts
- Detailing at bust, tummy or hip area
- Flounces or gathers at waist area
- Gathered or tiered skirts
- Clutch or shoulder bags
- Kitten heels, Ugg boots, ankle buckles, dainty shoes

Each and every single body-shape has its own attractive characteristics. To help dress the Apple shape, try to wear:

Neckline

- Lower and wider
- Scoop
- Square
- 'V'
- Sweetheart

Sleeves:

- Cap, if you have slim arms
- ¾ length
- Above the wrist
- Wrist length
- Flared
- Draped
- Shoulder pads ensure the clothes drape from widest part of shoulder

Tops and shirts:

- Simple lines
- Empire lines
- Styles that go in under the bust
- Open fronts
- Front or rear zips

Jackets:

- Single button under bust
- Empire or straight lines
- Deep neckline
- Wear open
- Shoulder pads

Coats:

- Cardigan style
- A Line
- Big lapels that sit at décolleté not bust
- Wear open
- Shoulder pads
- Vents in back

Dresses:

- A Line
- Dresses that draw attention away from tummy area

Skirts:

- Flip
- A Line
- Box pleats that sit below tummy
- Side fastening
- Side opening

Trousers:

- Flat front
- Wide leg
- Fasten on side
- Loose against body

Shoes:

- Chunky
- Medium to high heels
- Colourful
- Wedges
- Platforms

Bags:

Opt for handbags rather than shoulder bags. Try to choose medium to chunky.

Swim-Wear:

- Halter-neck
- Under-wired cups
- Thick straps
- Tankini
- Sarong
- Details at shoulder

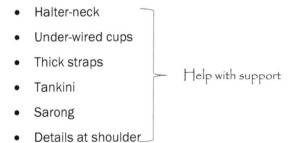

Help with support

Notes:

Lines and Shapes

The apple body shape is characterized by broad shoulders, a large bust, narrow hip, slim thighs, a flat rear end and an undefined waistline. Famous females with apple body shapes include Catherine Zeta-Jones, Tyra Banks, Elizabeth Hurley, Rosie O'Donnell and Angelina Jolie. Here's how to flaunt your best features by wearing clothing that draws attention away from your waist and creates balance.

Elongate your top. Find a V-neck that glides over your body and lengthens your top; this has a natural slimming effect. Don't go too tight or too loose, though.

Add a belt. Add slimming definition to your waist with a belt over a dress or long blouse.

Monochromatic outfits. Lengthen and slim your apple silhouette with the same color on top and bottom. Mix it up with varying shades of the same color and different fabric combinations.

Avoid tapered, tight bottoms. Boot-cut and flared jeans give a long and lean look. Too-tight and tapered jeans fail in creating a clean, straight line from the waist down.

Apple shapes carry extra weight in the stomach area but are smaller (or even skinny) on the top and bottom, often despite exercise and diet. The shape is extremely frustrating for

women who are self-conscious about their tummies and is especially common in pre- and postnatal women.

Lift & tuck.

Fashion experts recommend getting fitted for a great bra and purchasing some shapewear before you don any tops. This will help to keep your breasts lifted and the tummy smooth. Support is essential. With a full bust, a properly fitting bra can completely change your look, raising the bust line and narrowing the rib and waist area. Once you have all your body parts in place, it's easier to pick tops.

Don't be clingy.

We suggest wearing clothes that don't cling to the midriff area. Jersey materials and silks don't work well with the apple shape. You want to disguise problem areas, not draw attention to them. Patterns and textures help camouflage the weight in certain areas and are always on trend.

It's all about the A-line.

We also recommend a great A-line dress. Throw on a blazer to complete any look and hide problem areas. Shorter hemlines show off toned legs and help draw attention away from the stomach.

Skirts for Apples:

Women with apple body shapes are often well proportioned but tend to carry weight around their waist. Apple body shapes need to avoid adding volume to the midsection, while emphasizing their legs and breasts.

Stick to a structured skirt. You want non-flimsy fabric in a fitted -- not clingy -- cut.

Show some leg! Wearing skirts below-the-knee can feel dowdy, but styles that hit right at it are sexier and still feel chic. Pencil skirts with a flared hem are your best choice. Make sure to pair them with at least a 1-1/2 to 2-inch heel. The higher the heel the closer to the glam gods above.

Skirts with asymmetric hemlines or interesting detailing at the hem can also flatter this body type.

Figure Analysis... Inverted Triangle

Your shoulders are wide, tapering to a narrow hip, you have a straight rib cage and prefer a simpler look at the top. There is little definition between waist and hips, you have a flat bottom and hips, and also have a straight and squared shoulder line.

It is generally best to avoid wearing:

- Broadening necklines, such as
  - Bardot
  - Boat
  - Big straps
  - Halter necks
  - Shawls
  - Big collars
- Details at the shoulder
- Volume at shoulder
- Shoulder pads
- Puff sleeves
- Patterns on top
- Scarves
- Narrowing hemlines i.e. pencil skirts
- Clutch bags
- Dainty footwear

If you have gained and lost weight, your body shape may take on another shape. If you develop a larger bust, you can become an Apple, or if you are heavy, or have strong bones, you can become a Rectangle.

Corrective measures:

- Accentuate your hips
- Details in the lower half, keep top of body uncluttered
- Wear straight lines
- Use a wide belt to create a waist

The Inverted Triangle looks good wearing:

Neckline:

- Wide collars
- Lapels
- Bardot
- Boat

Sleeves:

- Slim lines
- No detailing

Tops and Shirts:

- Straight lines
- Wraps
- Splits on waist or hip
- Layering

Jackets:

- Straight, long lines
- Flared / full hemline
- Lower pockets
- Vents in back

Coats:

- Angular lines
- Long, tapered jackets
- Hip pockets
- Vents

Dresses:

- Simple, straight lines
- Shifts
- A Lines
- Full / tiered skirts
- Pleats
- Patterns
- Details

Skirts:

- A Line
- Tiered
- Volume
- Dropped waist
- Panels
- Pleats
- Boxed
- Vertical lines
- Full skirt
- Cn go from micro mini to long and flowing.

Trousers:

- Accentuate the bottom
- Details on pockets
- Pattern & print
- Combats
- Flares
- Cargo
- Palazzo
- Flares
- Culottes

Shoes:

- Detailed
- Wedges
- Platforms
- Chunky heels

- Ankle straps
- Ankle boots
- Uggs
- Cowboy boots

Bags:

Go for the bold, fussy, chunky detailed shoulder bags that sit at the hip or thigh.

Swim wear:

- One piece
- Halter-neck
- Hip detail

Notes:

Figure Analysis... Inverted triangle / Wedge

The Wedge is also known as the inverted triangle. This body shape features a broad upper body. The waist and hips are smaller in proportion, giving the body an inverted triangle or wedge body shape. You know you have a wedge body shape if your shoulders are the broadest part of your body.

If you have a wedge or inverted triangle body shape, you can count these celebrities as your style sisters; Renee Zellweger, Teri Hatcher, Demi Moore, Naomi Campbell, Catherine Zeta-Jones and Jennifer Garner all have wedge body shapes, characterized by broader upper bodies and narrow lower bodies.

How to dress a wedge-shaped body:

- Draw the eye down. Since a wedge body shape means your shoulders are the broadest part of your body, your style goal is to draw the eye downwards toward the narrower parts of your body, such as your waistline.
- Steer clear of strappy styles. Spaghetti strap styles draw attention to your shoulders -- a major no-no for wedge body shapes. Boat-necks and Bardot's are a style don't, too.
- Brighten up your bottom. Don't be afraid of wearing bright colors on your bottom half. Again, this draws the eye down to the narrowest part of your wedge body shape.
- Be 'waistful.' Create the illusion of a waist with a wide belt or by wearing high-waisted styles.

Wedge-shaped bodies typically feature bigger arms and busts than other body types. As with dressing for any body shape, the key is emphasizing your assets and playing down your liabilities. For example, turtlenecks are not a good choice. Even though your inclination might be to cover up the larger part of the body, turtlenecks just don't work for you. Instead, try V-necks and scoop necks that complement the larger bust.

Fashion experts love outfitting Wedge-shaped bodies. Show off the collarbones, draw the eye upwards. A wrap dress works great, and you can even throw a tank top underneath if it dips too low into the bust line. Short-sleeved blouses can be great but be careful. Don't wear a blouse that is too tight, pulls at the buttons and exposes your bra. Leave a couple buttons open at the top to accentuate the neckline and collarbone whilst drawing the eye down.

Accessorize.

Shorter necklaces complement most tops on a Wedge-shaped body. Stay away from longer necklaces, as they can get caught in the bust. A great pair of earrings goes a long way.

Flirty skirts for wedges

Fuller skirts balance out a wedge body shape. The wedge (also called the inverted triangle or strawberry) has broad shoulders and narrow hips. With this body shape, be sure to steer clear of pencil skirts and other body-hugging styles.

Stand tall and proud because you ladies have those squared off shoulders that command attention. The perfect skirts for you are those that flare, as these will help balance your broad shoulders.

Don't be afraid to experiment with bold colors and interesting patterns, they will draw the attention away from your upper body. Skirts with thigh high slits can also help balance a wedge shape body. It is generally best to avoid skirts that are high-waisted.

Celebrity wedges

Charlize Theron, Renee Zellweger, Jessica Simpson and Angelina Jolie are just some of the celebrities with wedge body shapes.

Notes:

Figure analysis Pencil / Lean

You are slim with narrow hips, waist and shoulder, your bust is small and high. You wear the same size on top and bottom, have little waist definition and have a flat hip and bottom area.

If you have gained and lost weight, your body shape may change toward another. You will be leaning toward a Pear if you become heavier in the hips. If you become slightly wider in the shoulder, you will be becoming an Inverted Triangle and if you have a larger bone structure and medium bust, you will find yourself in the Rectangle body shape.

Corrective measures:

Avoid wearing:

- Figure hugging clothes
- Long, straight and fitted lines in dresses, trousers and sleeves
- Tops and dresses with square necklines
- Shapeless jackets that hang loosely from the shoulder.
- Double breasted jackets
- Bulky, heavy textures
- Dropped waistlines

You will be trying to create an illusion of curves, for a more feminine look, so to that end, try:

- Layering to shorten your top half
- Create roundness and curves with tulip, gathers and peplum shapes
- Wear high waisted skirts and trousers to shorten your top half
- Broaden shoulders with shoulder pads
- Highlight hips with pockets and pleats

Neckline:

- Flexible.
- Ruffles
- Cowl
- Pussy bow
- Collars
- Neck ties
- Turtle neck
- Scoop neck

Places focus on centre of body

Sleeves:

- Batwing
- Dropped
- Flared
- Cuffed
- ¾ length
- Loose
- Short

Tops and Shirts:

- Empire line
- Yolk line
- Layering
- Wrap tops
- Push up bras
- Breast pockets
- Padded tops
- Pattern
- Detail

- Scarves
- Shawls

Jackets:

- Waisted
- Belted
- Pockets
- Shoulder detail
- Wide lapels
- Vents
- Single or double breasted
- Shoulder pads

Coats:

- Trench coats
- Single or double breasted
- Belted

Dresses:

- Princess line
- Empire line
- Curved darts
- Details
- Wraps

Skirts:

- A Line
- Pencil
- Flip
- Bias
- Wrap

Trousers:

- Shaped
- Pleated
- Pocketed
- Narrowing / tapered leg
- Culottes
- Capris
- Shorts
- Turn ups
- Side pockets

Shoes:

- Kitten heels
- Strappy
- Medium heels
- Ankle straps
- Boots
- Uggs
- Cowboy boots
- Rounded toe

Bags:

Opt for rounder shaped bags with soft edges, or medium sized clutch bags.

Swim wear:

Vertical chevrons give the illusion of shape, whilst patterned and padded styles also work well. A patterned two piece can be flattering.

Lines and Shapes

Your best assets are undoubtedly our arms and legs. You're lucky you don't have to minimize any body features!

Goals: To show off your slender arms and legs, define your waist and create curves!

Jackets and Blazers:

Avoid boxy styles. Jackets are best when they hit high hip bone and nip in at the waist for shape. Tailored trenches and belted jackets will give shape and define your waist and hips. You'll look best in classic single-breasted but you have one of the rare body types to rock a double-breasted jacket.

Tops:

Wear scoop neck and sweetheart tops to create curves. Also tops with collars, ruffles and details will flatter and enhance your chest. Choose high necklines for petite frames to elongate your body.

Dresses:

Your body looks amazing in shift dress because of your proportions and slender frame. You will look equally great in bias cut dresses just below the knee. Also, dresses with ruching or that cinch on the sides to create curves will work.

Skirts:

If you're looking to give the illusion of more curves, choose skirts which flare at the bottom to give you a girly shape. Styles with cinched waists and volume are perfect to make your hips look a little fuller. A-line skirts and tulip skirts are also curve-creating options. Pencil skirts will look great on you as well.

Trousers:

The best way to create curves on a straight bottom is by wearing something tight but not constricting. Flat front, semi low rise, skinny jeans, etc. all look great on you.

Tips & Tricks:

Layer to add more dimension. - Wear a good bra that will make the most of what you have.

Don't wear a V-neck alone. Tight V-necks over-elongate the body.

Stick with blouses and shirts with more detailing. Leave plain t-shirts, camisoles and solid tanks as a second layer. –

Stray from extremely full or baggy trousers. - Avoid straight, boxy mini-skirts.

Figure Analysis... Rectangle

Like the pencil, you have straight lines with no discernible waist, hips or bust to break up the line.

- You wear the same size top and bottom,
- Have a smaller bust,
- No discernible waist
- Flat hips and bottom.
- You have a straight shoulder to rib cage
- Straight hips and bottom
- Average tummy.

If you have gained and lost weight, your body shape may change. You will lean toward the Pear shape if you have a heavier bottom and thigh. If your shoulders become wider than your hips, you will become the Inverted Triangle and you will lean towards the Column if you have a smaller bust and stature.

There are some things it is best to avoid wearing, such as:

- Details at waist
- High waistband
- High-waisted trousers
- Belted jackets
- Pin stripes
- Straight lines
- Boxy jackets and coats
- Fussy, droopy or busy styles

- Rectangle shaped bags
- Square toes

Corrective measures:

- Create illusion of a waist
- Keep silhouette uncluttered
- Wear unstructured jackets to shape the waist
- Use hip and bottom details

A Rectangle generally looks good wearing:

Neckline:

- Lower and wider
- Jewels
- Scooped
- Boat-neck
- Use embellishments about the décolletage

Sleeves:

- Loose fit
- Puffed
- Cap
- ¾ length
- Flared
- Cuffed
- Rolled up

Tops and Shirts:

- Simple, clean lines
- Rounded at neckline
- Empire line
- Draping under bust
- Movement
- Split at waist

Jackets:

- Structured and shaped
- Round lapels
- Round neckline

Coats:

- Straight lines
- Emphasis on the waist
- Empire lines
- Uncluttered

Dresses:

- Kaftans
- Straight lines
- Simple
- Empire lines
- Shift dresses

Skirts:

- Crossover
- Flip
- Panelled
- A Line

Trousers:

- Flexible
- Low waisted
- Boot cut
- Flared
- Wide leg
- Hip or thigh detail
- Pockets
- Pleats
- Turn ups

Shoes:

- Round or oval toe
- Mary Janes
- Ugg boots
- Ballerinas

Bags:

Go for the straighter styles such as rectangular or clutch bags.

Swim Wear:

- Form fitting waist
- Soft cup bra
- 2 pieces
- Solid, bold colours
- Plunging necklines
- Diagonal lines
- One piece with dark waist area
- Tankini

Notes:

Lines and shapes

Rectangle-shaped celebs: Natalie Portman, Cameron Diaz, Kate Hudson, Hilary Swank

- o Rectangle body traits: The waist, hip and shoulder widths are similar and are usually on the slim side. Slender rectangles have an athletic look about them.
- o Your best assets: Your arms and legs — and you don't have to minimize any body features.
- o Your fashion goals: Create curves and show off slender legs and arms.

Dos and don'ts

If your body is rectangle-shaped like Natalie Portman's, then you want to create curves where they don't necessarily exist.

- o DO wear scoop neck and sweetheart tops to create curves.
- o DO wear long jackets to create a lean look.
- o DO wear tops with collars, ruffles and details to flatter your chest.
- o DO wear a good bra that will make the most of what you have.
- o DON'T wear overwhelming styles.
- o DO layer to add more dimensions.
- o DO wear dresses with ruching. Cinches on sides are ideal.
- o DO have fun with colorful bottoms... feel free to experiment.

Rectangle body shapes are straight up and down without a defined waist. To give the illusion of more curves, choose skirts that provide a 'girly' shape.

Skirts for rectangles

Any trim that has flounce or ruffle is fantabulous. Try to keep the skirt's overall shape close to the body as this way the skirt doesn't overwhelm your trim little body. Another option is to choose a skirt that flares. A cinched waist and a style with volume are the perfect way to make hips look, better balanced. A-line skirts and tulip skirts are also curve-creating options.

Celebrity rectangles

Gwyneth Paltrow, Keira Knightley, Reese Witherspoon, Kate Hudson, Nicole Richie and many models have rectangle body shapes.

Figure Analysis... Hourglass

Your bust and hips are wider than your waist, giving you the classic hourglass shape. You have:

- Clearly defined waist
- Clearly defined bust
- Curved bottom
- Wear the same size top and bottom.

If you have lost and gained weight, your body shape can change. Carrying extra weight around the hips will give you a Pear shape. Extra weight about the waist will create an Apple and a fuller bust, hip and tummy will give you a Fuller Hourglass.

It is best to avoid wearing any style or shape that hides your body, as this will add volume to your waist.

Corrective measures:

In order to create visual balance:

- Wear shaped and fitted lines
- Follow your body line
    - Define the waist
    - Enhance the bust
    - Highlight hip and bottom

This is the classically feminine shape and is very flexible when it comes to dressing it. Try to stick to the following.

Neckline:

Very flexible as long as you don't have a short or wide neck.

Sleeves:

The choice is limitless, they all work for you.

Tops and Shirts:

- Very versatile
- Wraps
- Fitted
- Waistcoats
- Layering
- Crossovers

Jackets:

- Fitted shapes with waist definition
- Shoulder pads
- Double breasted
- Empire line
- Lapels
- Breast or hip pockets

Coats:

All shapes as long as they have some shape at the waist or a belt.

Dresses:

Any style, either shaped, belted, short or long will flatter you

Skirts:

- Very flexible
- A Line
- Pencil
- Panelled
- Flip
- Dropped waist
- Bias cut
- Pleats
- Waistbands
- Full skirts

Trousers:

- Very versatile
- Long
- Short
- Wide
- Narrow
- Pockets / none
- Pleats or plain front
- With or without turn-ups

Shoes:

- Very versatile
- Petite, medium detailing

Bags:

Any choice will suit you.

Swim wear:

There are again, no restrictions, just remember that the best styles are the ones that underline your shape and femininity.

Notes:

Lines and shapes

When dressing to flatter your hourglass shaped figure, your main challenge will be to maintain the look of the ideal shape that you already have. Avoid styles, such as shifts or trapeze dresses that hide your shape.

Also avoid styles that tend to over-emphasize either bust or hips. For example, if you wear a gathered skirt, your hips will look bigger and make you look bottom-heavy. Paying attention to style and cut in the garments you buy pays off when your clothing flatters your ideal hourglass figure shape by following your natural curves.

So even though a garment may be the latest trendy item, think twice before buying any clothing that hides your lovely shape.

Your other big challenge will be to find clothing that fits you well. Because most manufacturers cut their clothing for women who have triangle or sometimes rectangle shapes, you will often find that a dress that fits well in the bodice does not fit well in the hip area. Consider:

- Wearing separates to attain a better fit.
- Finding a dressmaker who can custom fit your clothes.
- Becoming expert at fitting if you sew.

Select shoes without ankle straps and have your dress hemmed shorter to just graze the bottom of your knees, both of these would help make you look taller.

The benefits of an hourglass figure are: sexy, curvy proportions and defined waist.

The problem on the other hand is: tendency to look heavy and short (because of your broad hips). Defining the waist and lengthening your legs will do the trick.

All an hourglass woman needs to do, is dress in clothes that follow the curves of their body shape rather than hide it. Clothes that follow the curves of your hourglass body will make you appear balanced and feminine.

You can see that in the samples below. The pieces without a defined waistline (straight orange line) will hide your curves. To make sure your waistline is visible you have to make sure you wear tailored (form fitting) clothes.

One of the most important rules for an hourglass figure is to make sure the waistline is defined and not hidden. If you want even more curves, add volume equivalently to your

upper and lower body – but do not just add volume to just the top or just the bottom as that would put your body out of balance.

Make sure your clothes are snug but not clingy. Rather go one size up in a form-fitting style than have your clothes pull at your figure.

Avoid tops, jackets and dresses with straight lines, since they cover your curves and will make you appear heavy.

Fabrics for hourglass figures

Textured, stiff and thick fabrics cannot follow the curves of your body, so avoid fabrics like structured linen, denim, chunky knits, corduroy, twill, thick jersey or Thai silk.

Exception: Skirts in A-line are great in a structured fabric, as the fabric ensures that the skirt keeps its form. Make sure the skirt fits well in the waist.

Fabrics that are great for hourglass body shape women include denim with elastane, fine jersey, very fine cotton or cotton mixed with elastane / polyester, fine knits and fine silk.

Dress the beautiful hourglass body shape:

Neckline styles:

Necklines that are slightly rounded look great on you, as the oval, deep oval, rounded or jewel neckline. You can also wear V-necks, sweethearts and scoop necks.

Avoid wide necklines like square and boat necks as well as high necklines and turtlenecks if you are busty; they will make you look top-heavy.

Collar styles

Light ruffles can look great for an hourglass figure if you want to add volume. You can only wear big ruffles if you are small breasted, otherwise they would add too much volume. Classic lapels are also great on you.

Sleeve styles

Your clothes should follow your natural curve, so go for set-in sleeves. They are perfect for your sloping shoulders. Shoulder seams should be precisely at the joint where the arm attaches.

You can dress in short sleeves to sleeves above the elbow. For long sleeves opt for fitted ones or flowing bishop sleeves. If you want to show some of your femininity, ensure that the sleeves do not cover the complete curve of the wrist.

Hourglass figures can wear small shoulder pads but should avoid large ones. With a sleeveless look you can show off your beautiful rounded shoulders.

Tops & Shirts

An hourglass figure has a beautiful waist; make sure your tops show off this great asset. Tops, blouses and shirts should be fitted. They should nip in at the waist without adding bulk to your chest. Also avoid big ruffles, bows or any other embellishments that would add a lot of volume to you top (unless you add some volume to your hips to balance that out). Extra bulk on your chest will throw your proportions out of sync and extra bulk on your waist would hide your waist's natural curve.

If you wear a turtleneck, make sure the collar is pretty small. Otherwise you might look very busty.

Wrap tops are great as they show your waist without adding extra volume to your chest.

Soften or accentuate your curves?

If you want to downplay your curves, put on a top in dark or muted colors or in vertical stripes. The top should end just below your hipbone or past your thighs.
If you want to show off your curves, opt for a top in light or bright colors or big print. A top that stops just short of your waist is great for highlighting your feminine top half.

Tip: Always wear a well-fitting, supportive bra to lift and tame your bust.

T-Shirt styles

The T-Shirt for an hourglass body shape should be form-fitting. This accentuates your waist and should end at or above your hips.

Jackets

Always go for jackets that follow your body line and draw in toward the waist. Look for form-fitting and belted jackets. If your jacket does not come with a belt, just add one around the waist. Short jackets that stop just above your hips accentuate your curves in a flattering way.

Avoid straight and boxy styles as they do not show your waist and thus make you appear heavier. A slim waistline is the defining feature of an hourglass figure so try and avoid anything that hides it!

Coats

Form-fitting coats are great, look for fitted A-line coats, trench-coats and long coachmen styles. If your coat has embellishments around your bust, make sure you have enough volume around your hips for balance. Puff-sleeves or epaulettes to emphasize your shoulders are great.

Empire lines do look great on you. Having the waist at your natural waistline will look even better though. Flaunt what you've got!

Avoid drop waist coats as they hide your natural waistline. Boxy and straight coat styles also hide your waist, for some adding a belt works – for some coats that adds too much bulk around your waist, try it out and decide for yourself.

Wrap dresses are perfect for hourglass figures as they show off your waistline.

Dresses for an hourglass figure

Your best bet are dresses that draw the focus to your waist without adding extra volume to your bust. Wrap dresses do just that. Tailored sheaths, t-shirt dresses, wrap, bias and strapless dresses are really cute on hourglass shaped women.

If you want to appear more curvaceous, add volume both to bust and hip through ruffles, embellishments or pockets.

If you want to downplay your curves, look for a dress in dark colors or vertical stripes.

Do not hide your figure in shapeless dresses! It might take some courage to show off your sexy curves; if you are not sure,

take some pictures before you leave the house or ask friends.

Skirts for an hourglass figure

Skirts are best high-waisted, as low-waisted ones only add bulk to your lower half. You can dress in A-line, full circle, pencil, tulip and gored skirts in medium and long; knee length skirts will be your best bet though. These skirts hug your hips and hang off them naturally. Short straight skirts will look great under a top or jacket. You probably have great legs, so show them off. Show those rectangle fashion models what a real hourglass body shape can look like

Look for skirt materials that stretch or drape. Stiff and thick materials make your hips look boxy and wider than they actually are. Only wear stiff materials with an A line skirt that shows your tiny waist.

If you want to emphasize your hip curves, you can go for a skirt with a peplum. But be aware, it might add too much volume.

Avoid skirts with big voluminous pockets, ruffles or other embellishments around your hip unless you balance them with details around your chest. Keep away from darts.

Trousers

Trousers that start above or below your stomach are great. Your best bet would be wide-legged and loose-fitting trousers that go straight down to the floor. Hourglass types also look great in slightly tapered, boot-cut or flare out trousers. The flare retains the portion of your lower leg, in balance with your hips.

Avoid pleats/darts in trousers as your tummy curves tend to cause pleats to lay open. Also keep away from big voluminous pockets around your hip. You do not want to add extra volume here. Skip baggy pants, they are too bulky for your feminine curves.

Your trousers should have flat fronts and pockets without flaps or large buttons. You should also avoid decorative embellishments or other decorations at the hip. In case you have to wear them make sure you keep an hourglass figure. This means you have to add something to your top as well to avoid appearing unbalanced.

Straight leg and boot-cut jeans will make a sporty look paired with a figure hugging shirt.

Mid- or high-rise trousers are fabulous as they elongate your legs. They should lay flat on your belly. Jeans with wide waist-bands are great for hourglass shaped women. Wide-legged, loose fitting, slightly tapered, boot-cut and flared jeans styles are great.

Skinny jeans could make you look shorter, so pair them with a balanced top and high heels that add extra length to your leg. Look for jeans with stretch denim as this fabric will be able to follow your curves.

Avoid low-rise pants. They make your hips look wider and your legs look shorter.

Jumpsuits

You can wear belted and form-fitting jumpsuit styles. Just make sure that the leg is not too tapered.

Avoid too many details at the hip as the biggest strength of an hourglass body shape is the even distribution on hip and shoulders. Putting too much attention on either hip or shoulder-line will counter that effect and reduce the strength of your waistline.

Swimwear & Beachwear

You can sport a wide variety of one-piece and two-piece swimsuits. Strapless and bandeau tops look great on hourglass shaped women. For a large bust, opt for halter tops, string bikinis with sufficient coverage and support. If you like to appear more curvaceous, buy one with ruffles, padding and embellishments. Bottoms should cut straight across your hips.

You can choose any color or pattern; just keep away from big differences in color between top and bottom as this will put your body out of balance.

Have fun with accessories

Especially when they look feminine and rounded.

Make sure belts follow the natural curve of your waistline. Small to medium size belts and soft belts are great for that. Be aware of wide belts, as they can make an hourglass body shape with a small torso look even smaller. Be careful with hip belts as they emphasize your bottom and might make it more voluminous.

Short necklaces that hug your neck or long necklaces in a V-form are great. Keep away from very angular necklaces and necklaces that hang too low and wide over your chest, especially if they hit just below the breast. Necklaces that reach your belly are fine.

Shoe styles for an hourglass body shape

Classic shoes like court shoes with medium heel are great as well as kitten heels. For hot days, choose a sandal with closed-in toe and a simple strap around the heel. Pointy-toed or almond toe shoes with trousers that are wide at the hem are great for hourglass shaped women because they elongate the leg-line. Round toed shoes are good as well, just wear your trousers very long (almost skimming the ground).

Heels are made for you! Even if you wear just a little heel that will help to elongate your legs and show off your femininity.

Look for a boot with a medium heel that is snug to your leg.

An hourglass figure should avoid straight leg boots as they cover the curves of your ankles as well as above-the-knees and calf-length boots.

Bag styles for an hourglass figure

To play down your curves, choose a bag with angles. E.g.: a structured Satchel, a boxy Cigar Box, a classic or a geometric clutch. To celebrate your body shape, choose a bag with curves, e.g. soft Pouch, an oval bag, a soft and slouchy Hobo, a long and rounded Baguette, or a semi-circular clutch. Shoulder straps on bags are uncomfortable for you because of your sloping shoulders. They will tend to slide off your shoulders.

The form of your bag is important, but size matters as well. As a petite hourglass, would be better choosing a small bag. As a large hourglass figure, choose a bigger bag.

Notes:

Determining Your Face Shape

There are a few approaches to this. You will need...

- A mirror large enough to see your whole face
- It may help to have a photo of your face. Pull your hair back away from your face and make sure the photo is taken square-on to your face, so you can see both sides. If you're taking the photo yourself, for example with a cell phone

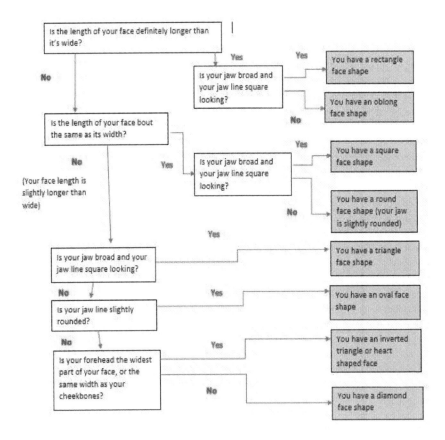

camera, make sure the camera is far enough away that you don't get a distorted, fish-eye effect!

- Or, it may help to draw the outline of your face, with your hair held away from your face, on the mirror (make sure whatever you use -- for example, whiteboard marker, eye-liner pencil, lipstick -- will wipe off later!)

Ok, now you're ready to fine tune the shape of your face by answering these questions:

You may discover it's not as easy as you'd think to categorize the shape of your face. Each of us has a unique face length-width ratio, jaw, jaw-line and front-on outline. So, it's not always a cut-and-dry decision as to which face shape category to choose.

For example, if your face length is definitely longer than wide and you have a broad, square jaw-line then, using the questionnaire above, you will come out as a rectangle. However, if, when looking at your front-on outline (the sides of your face), your jaw is the widest part of your face the triangle category may be a better choice for you. It will depend how much your face is longer than wide; do you see your face length first? Or is your jaw more obvious than your face length? Another approach is to combine the recommendations for both shapes.

My face shape is:

Your Rectangular Face Shape

Your forehead, cheek and jaw are all a similar width.

Your main style aims are...

To create the illusion of a shorter, broader face and to soften your jaw-line.

Hairstyles

Go for...

- Natural looking styles
- Styles that add width at your temples
- Styles that add width at your cheekbones
- Styles that add a little volume (not too much) at the top of your head
- If you have a high forehead, bangs (a fringe) are good
- Either straight and wispy or swept off to the side and not too thick
- Keep the sides off your face, either swept back or short
- Off centre or side parting
- Medium length is good

- Long hair should add width at the neckline

Avoid...

- Highly stylised styles such as angular cuts, extremely short styles, severely slicked down
- Volume only on top of your head
- Middle parting
- Long straight hair all the same length
- Hair close to the sides of your face
- If you have a high forehead, hair combed straight back

Glasses (Eyeglasses and Sunglasses)

The best glasses for your face shape are...

- Frames with depth as well as width
- Frames slightly wider than your face
- Frames with curves rather than sharp angles
- Contrasting colour or decoration at the temple
- If your nose is long, avoid a low bridge

Hats

- Hats with full brims
- Uplifted brims
- Avoid high crowns and small brims that make your face look longer

Makeup Tips

Add the appearance of width at your cheekbones and the illusion of a shorter face by...

- Applying a slightly darker foundation at your hairline around your forehead and just under and slightly over your jaw
- Applying a slightly darker foundation just under your cheekbones, blend towards the ear
- Applying a blusher on the apple (ball) of your cheekbones and blend upwards towards the outer corner of your eye

Earrings

Your best earrings have more width than depth and soft curves, rather than angles. Such as...

- Round buttons
- Tear drops
- Ovals

- If you have long hair, drops no longer than your chin and with some width too.

These celebrities have your shaped face...

- Sandra Bullock
- Lucy Liu
- Ted Danson

Notes:

Your Oblong Face Shape.

Your face shape is obviously longer than it is wide with a square jaw-line. You may also have a square hairline.

Main characteristics...

- Your face is definitely longer than wide
- Your jaw-line is softly rounded
- The sides of your face are straight -- your forehead, cheekbones and jaw-line are the same width
- Your hairline may be rounded

Your main style aims are...

To make your face appear shorter and broader.

Hairstyles for Your Face Shape

Go for...

- Styles that add a little height and width at the temples and cheekbones
- Length medium-short to medium long
- Short styles are best when tapered in from the eye-line into the nape of the neck
- Longer hair needs volume in the neck area

- Hair off the sides, either short, or swept back or behind the ears
- Soft, natural looking layers
- If your forehead is high, wispy or open bangs (fringe)
- Off centre parting

Avoid...

- Long hair all the same length
- Very short hair
- Centre partings
- Hair close to your temple

Eyeglasses and Sunglasses for Your Face Shape

Your best styles have the following characteristics...

- Frames with depth as well as width to make your face appear shorter
- Decorative or contrasting temples
- A low bridge to shorten a long nose

Hats

- Full or upturned brims
- Not too much height in the crown

Makeup Tips

- Apply darker foundation at the hairline around the forehead
- Apply darker foundation over the chin
- Apply darker foundation in the hollows of your cheeks
- Apply blush on the apple (ball) of your cheekbones and blend out towards the top of your ear

Earrings

- Your best earrings have more width than length
- Round, square and fan
- Teardrops
- Small hoops
- Drops no longer than the chin, better with some width.

Celebrities with an Oblong Shaped Face:

- Sarah Jessica Parker,
- Cate Blanchett

- Kate Winslett
- Michael Parkinson,
- Tom Cruise
- Russell Crow

Notes:

Your Oval Face Shape

- Your face is slightly longer than wide
- Your jaw-line is slightly rounded
- The outline of your face is an inverted egg-shape -- your face is widest at the cheekbones. Your forehead is fairly broad (broader than you jaw)
- Your face can be divided into 3 equal horizontal sections between the hairline, eyebrows, end of nose and chin
- Your eyes are evenly spaced, with one eye width distance between them
- Your face has no extreme characteristics. For example, you do not have very small or very large eyes, mouth or nose.

Your face has the pleasing, balanced shape of an inverted egg, with well-proportioned eyes, nose and mouth.

Lucky you! You have the perfect face shape!

The main style aim for all other face shapes is to become more like yours! Most styles will suit you. You only need general style guidelines, rather than face shape correction tips.

Your main style aims are...

To choose styles that fit your lifestyle and personality.

Haircuts for Oval Face Shape

You can choose almost any hairstyle and length. Your main considerations are...

- Styles that suit the texture, curl and quantity of your hair
- If you are over 40 its best to keep the length on or above shoulder length and to choose styles that sweep hair away from the face

Eyeglasses and Sunglasses for Your Face Shape

Choose styles that are...

- In proportion with the size of your head. For example, if you have a small head wear glasses with smaller frames and vice versa
- As wide as, or slightly wider than, the widest part of your face
- Update your glasses every 2 to 3 years with a current style

Hats

Many hat styles will suit you. However, your best styles...

- Have large brims that are either floppy or straight and no wider than your shoulders
- Keep your <u>body height and scale</u> in mind and choose hats in proportion. For example, if you are short or have a small bone structure your hats should not be too large

Makeup Tips

You can have fun experimenting with different makeup styles. Remember the basic rules...

- When applying foundation, blush and eye shadow, light shades make areas appear more prominent and darker shades decrease the apparent size of the area
- Apply blush just under the apple (ball) of your cheek-bone and fade in a smooth arc towards the top of your ear

Earrings

Most shapes of earrings will suit your face shape. Choose...

- Earrings in proportion with your head size and body scale
- Update your styles regularly as an easy and inexpensive way to update your look and remain contemporary

Famous people with your face shape include...

- Halle Berry
- Madonna,

Notes:

Your Diamond Face Shape

Main characteristics...

- Your face is slightly longer than wide
- Your jaw-line is long and pointed
- Your cheekbones are the widest part of your face. They are often high and pointed
- Your forehead and jaw-line are tapered
- Your eyes, nose and mouth are well balanced vertically

Your face is widest at the cheekbones and narrow at both the chin and forehead. Therefore, your main style aims are...

To create the illusion of a broader chin and forehead:

Hairstyles

Go for...

- Styles that are full at your temples and chin
- Hair close to your head in the cheekbone area
- Slightly off-centre parting
- Fringe that sweep to the side
- Medium length styles
- Hair swept up into an up-do
- Styles with symmetrical lines

Avoid...

- Very short styles
- Centre parting
- Styles that add fullness at your cheeks
- Close hair cut at your temples
- Too much volume at the top of your head

Glasses

The best glasses for your face shape are...

- No wider than your cheekbones
- Frames with soft curves such as oval shapes
- Styles that add width at the brow, for example, with decoration or colour at the top of the frame
- Frames that are narrower on the bottom and wider at the top such as cat-eye shapes

Hats

Choose hats that make your forehead appear broader. For example, hats with large brims.

Makeup Tips

- Apply a slightly lighter shade of foundation at your temples and jaw-line to make them appear broader

- Apply blush to the apple (ball) of your cheek, no lower than the bottom of your nose, and blend towards the centre of your ear

Earrings

Choose shapes that add width to your jaw-line. Your best shapes are narrower at the top and wider at the bottom, such as...

- Tear drops
- Pear shapes
- Triangle shapes
- Ovals

You share a face shape with Elizabeth Hurley.

Notes:

Your Triangle or Pear Face Shape

Main characteristics...

- Your face is slightly longer than wide
- Your jaw is broad
- The side of your face tapers from your jaw to your forehead

Your face is broad and square at the jaw-line, tapering to a relatively narrow forehead.

If your jaw-line is rounded, rather than square, you have a pear face shape.

Your main style aims are...

To minimise your jaw-line and add width at your temples.

Hairstyles for Your Triangle Face Shape

Go for...

- Styles that add a little height and width at the temples
- Cover part or all of the ears
- Keep hair close to the head at the jaw-line
- Side parting
- Irregular layers and wispy styles
- Long bangs (fringe) swept to the side
- Full and fluffy fringe

Avoid...

- Adding width at the jaw-line
- Centre parting
- Hair close to the temples
- Very short on top

Glasses

Your best styles have the following characteristics...

- Frames that have design detail and colour at the top of the frame
- Frames that are heavy at the top
- Frames with cat-eye or oval shapes
- Frames slightly wider than your temples

Hats

- Any style that adds width at the forehead
- Asymmetric brims and crowns with some height are good to draw attention upwards

Makeup Tips

- Apply a darker shade of foundation on the chin and jaw areas
- Apply a lighter shade of foundation at the sides of your forehead
- Apply blush from the apple (ball) of your cheekbones in a V shape towards your temples

- Wear earrings that are longer than they are wide
- Avoid triangular shapes

Famous people with your face shape include...

- Billie Piper
- Minnie Driver

Notes:

Your Inverted Triangle or Heart Face Shape

The only difference between the inverted triangle and the heart shaped faces are that the heart has a widow's peak.

Main characteristics...

- Your face is slightly longer than wide
- Your jaw-line is long and pointed
- The sides of your face taper from your forehead to your jaw
- Your forehead is the widest part of your face, or the same width as your cheekbones
- Your jaw is the narrowest part of your face

Your main style aims are...

...To make your forehead appear narrower and add width at your jaw-line and chin.

Hairstyles for Your Face Shape

Go for...

- Hairstyles that are close to your face above your ears, with soft lines partially covering your ears
- Centre parting
- A soft style with light bangs (fringe) covering your forehead

- Soft waves and curly styles
- Styles that add volume at the jaw-line

Avoid...

- Pulling your hair back off your forehead
- Styles that are full at the temples
- Straight bangs (fringe)
- Too much height on top of your head
- A low side parting

Glasses

The best glasses for your face shape are...

- Frames that add width below your eye-line
- Round or oval frames with soft curves or an upward sweep
- Low arms
- Light to medium coloured frames and rimless styles
-

Hats

- Look for hats with a prominent crown to make your forehead appear narrower
- Wear a hat on an angle

Makeup

- Apply a slightly darker shade of foundation at the temples to make your forehead appear narrower

- Apply a light shade of foundation on either side of the jaw-line to make your jaw-line appear wider
- Apply blush to the apple (ball) of your cheek and blend towards the centre of your ear

Earrings

Add length to your face and width to your jaw-line by choosing the following shapes...

- Drops
- Teardrops
- Rectangles
- Ovals

These famous people have your shape face...

- The Dixie Chicks' Natalie Maines
- Andrew Denton

Notes:

Your Square Face Shape

Main characteristics...

- Your face is almost as wide as it is long
- Your jaw is broad and your jaw-line is square
- The sides of your face are straight -- your forehead, cheekbones and jaw are the same width
- Your hairline is most probably straight

Your main style aims are...

To create the illusion of a longer face and maybe, to soften your jaw-line.

Face Shape Hair Styles

Go for...

- Styles that add height to the top of the head
- Curve and angle hair across the forehead
- An off-centre parting
- Soft, layered styles
- Wisps, curls and waves
- Broken and asymmetric styles
- Hair close to ears to emphasize the cheekbones

Avoid...

- Very straight styles
- Styles that add width to your jaw-line

Eyeglasses and Sunglasses for Your Face Shape

Your best styles have the following characteristics...

- Narrow oval frames or frames with narrow frames and upward curves to minimize the square-ness of your face
- Frames wider than they are deep to make your face appear longer
- Colour or decoration on the upper outer corners of the frame
- Frames no wider than the width of your face

Hats

- An irregular brim and a prominent crown will make your face appear longer
- Wear at an angle to soften your face's square-ness

Face Shape Makeup Tips

- Minimise and soften your forehead and jaw-line by applying a darker shade of foundation at your temples and jaw
- Apply blush on the apple (ball) of your cheekbone and blend towards the top of your ear. Most of the colour should be on the apple of your cheekbone

- Wear earrings that are longer than they are wide

Notes:

Your Round Face Shape

Main characteristics...

- Your face is almost as wide as it is long
- Your jaw-line is round and full
- Your cheekbones are the widest part of your face and round
- Your hairline is most probably round

Your main style aims are...

To create the illusion of a longer, slimmer face.

Hairstyles for Your Round Face Shape

Go for...

- Styles that add height to the top of the head
- Hair off the face, but close to the head
- Centre or long diagonal parting
- Short to long hair
- Layers
- Styles that end just below the chin, or with layers ending below your chin
- Gently waves
- Wispy ends

Avoid...

- Styles that add width
- Round styles
- Straight bangs (fringe)
- Very short hair
- Very curly hair
- Very straight hair

Glasses

Your best styles have the following characteristics...

- Frames wider than high to make your face appear longer
- Frames no wider than the width of your face
- Frames with angles rather than curves

Hats

Make your face appear longer by choosing hats with...

- An irregular brim
- A prominent crown
- Vertical design features such as feathers

Makeup Tips

Make your face appear narrower and add more definition by...

- Applying a darker shade of foundation in an arc on either side of your forehead
- Applying a darker shade of foundation on either side of your jaw, blending up to the tip of your ear
- Apply blush just under the apple (ball) of your cheeks and extend to your temples

Earrings

Wear earrings longer than they are wide, for example rectangle drops look good on you.

These famous people have your face shape...

- Kirsten Dunst
- Pauline Quirk
- Paul Merton

Notes:

What's my style?

Now that we know our horizontal body type, body shape and face shape, we need to develop our own unique style.

Stand in front of a full-length mirror and critically evaluate yourself. This does not mean be mean. This means really, truly think about what you are seeing. Pretend you are a complete stranger and see yourself through their eyes, let the ideas flow through you.

If you saw yourself on the street, what clothes / style would you be wearing? Try not to let your current choices cloud your imagination. Do you look like a dress and heels kind of person? Or maybe a jeans and T-Shirt? Are you formal? Informal? Casual? Dressy? Are you modest? A little more risqué? What do your friends, family, partner think you would look good in? You will be surprised how long they have been waiting to help you.

Find a recent photograph of yourself and cut round the head. Then find a magazine or catalogue and put your photograph over the heads of models with similar body shapes to you. Yep, I know it's daft, but it does help you to get an idea of what you would look like in outfits and styles that you would perhaps never try.

Place your photograph over the most ridiculous outfits you can find, in colours that you would never dream of wearing. Surprise! Some of them actually suit you.

We get stuck in a style rut. The choices we made many years (and fashions) ago are just easier to keep buying and wearing. Who has time for change, right? Well, with just a few basics in our wardrobe, we can look good every day with very minimal effort. You are doing the hard part right now. Change is hard. But you recognised that you wanted a little change or you wouldn't have worked this far through the book. So, well done! Nearly there now, and the polished new you is just waiting to meet the world.

Back to the photograph. Nope, I haven't forgotten. Why not try your picture over styles from different ethnicities? Who is to say that the race we were born to is the only clothing style we should wear? Some cross-culture looks are stunning on women of all ages. After all, we are going for change... Right? Some of the fabrics, prints and cuts are breath-taking and would probably look awesome on you. Use your photograph and see for yourself.

Now that we have loosened up our ideas of what we could or couldn't be seen out in public in, we need to think about where we are wearing these new clothes. Are you a professional? A student? Stay at home mum? Lady that lunches? Each activity generally calls for its own 'uniform'. So, what is the dress code at work? What is functional, easy to wear and practical with the family? We need to assess the jobs our clothes will be doing and this will help us narrow the field even further. Do you have any medical conditions that can affect which clothes you wear? For instance, I have Fibromyalgia and Arthritis which means clothes hurt me, I have to wear things without waistbands, and no stiff or itchy fabrics.

I am sure that most of us have heard the term "Capsule Wardrobe". We are going to break that down into realistic terms that we can apply to our own busy lives. We need to write down the things we do on a daily basis, I.e.:

Stay at home mum:

	Morning	Lunch	Afternoon	Evening
Monday	School run / house-work	Lunch with friends	School run / Cook tea	Husband/ partner / cat
Tuesday	School run / etc	Home	Shopping	As above
Wednesday				
Etc.				

Working woman:

	Morning	Lunch	Afternoon	Evening
Monday	Meeting	Working lunch	Training	Restraunt
Tuesday	Travelling	Lunch meeting	Travelling	Office/Gym
Etc.				

This is a snapshot of 'a day in the life of...'

Create a similar one for yourself to get an idea of the type of outfits you will be needing.

	Morning	Lunch	Afternoon	Evening
Monday				
Tuesday				
Wednesday				
Thursday				
Friday				
Saturday				
Sunday				

Which activities are most often occurring? What type of clothes does this call for? Formal, casual, functional...? We also need to bear in mind how often we do the laundry. Every day? Weekly? This usually depends on the amount of people you are caring for.

Now that we have an idea of the clothes we need on a daily basis, let's put together that wardrobe.

Starting with the basics...

Under-wear	Separates	Casual	Formal / Work etc.
Bra x 7	Tops x 4	Tops x 4	Dresses x 2
Knickers x 7	Trousers x 2	Bottoms x 4	Suits x 2
Nightwear x 4	Skirts x 2	Dresses x 3	Tights/Stockings x 5
Tights/Socks x 7	Jackets x 2	Gym Clothes x 2	Jackets x 2
Footwear x 2	Coats x 1	Trainers x 1	Shoes x 2

Is there anything else that you need to add?

Create your own capsule wardrobe. Donate anything you haven't worn for 6 months to charity (season dependant). Or perhaps hold a Swishing party at home to refresh your clothes or accessories whilst preventing more landfill. Why not use the Notes pages at the end of the book to think of inexpensive ways of updating your wardrobe then share them on my Facebook page?   https://www.facebook.com/BeaMakeovers

One idea is to take the time to arrange your wardrobe with each outfit together, i.e. tops, bottoms, underwear, hosiery etc. This way you will always have an outfit sorted so that no matter how busy you are, you can just grab it and know you will look fabulous that day. Also, after they have been washed, they can go straight back into their slot, ready for the next time.

I hope that you have found this helpful. I know that change is scary, but you've gotten this far, so let's take the next step together... Please join my Facebook page and ask me any questions you like, I will do my very best to help you. Or, why not come along to one of the Feeling Fabulous Workshops that are currently in Essex, soon to be country wide.

I look forward to meeting you one day so that you can tell me all about how you have taken control of your wardrobe.

Take care and stay gorgeous

Notes:

Thank you for reading this, I hope you have found it of use.

Please feel free to follow me on:

Facebook https://www.facebook.com/BeaMakeovers,

Instagram QueenBeaMakeovers and **Linkdin** queen bea

27646661R00063

Printed in Poland
by Amazon Fulfillment
Poland Sp. z o.o., Wrocław